THE HALLOWEEN PARTY

CHOOSE YOUR OWN
NIGHTMARE...

titles in Large-Print Editions:

CHOOSE YOUR OWN

NIGHTMARE... #5

THE HALLOWEEN PARTY
BY E.A.M. JAKAB

ILLUSTRATED BY BILL SCHMIDT

An Edward Packard Book

Gareth Stevens Publishing
MILWAUKEE

For a free color catalog describing Gareth Stevens' list of high-quality books,
call 1-800-542-2595 (USA) or 1-800-461-9120 (Canada).
Gareth Stevens' Fax: (414) 225-0377.

Library of Congress Cataloging-in-Publication Data

Jakab, E. A. M.
    The Halloween party / by E. A. M. Jakab ; illustrated by
Bill Schmidt.
        p. cm. — (Choose your own nightmare)
    Summary: The reader's decisions control the course of adventures
at a Halloween party which is getting way out of hand and which
seems to be chaperoned by a witch.
    ISBN 0-8368-1514-9 (lib. bdg.)
    1. Plot-your-own stories. [1. Halloween—Fiction. 2. Adventure
and adventurers—Fiction. 3. Plot-your-own stories.] I. Schmidt, Bill,
ill. II. Title. III. Series.
PZ7.J153546Hal 1996
[Fic]—dc20   95-39818

This edition first published in 1996 by
Gareth Stevens Publishing
1555 North RiverCenter Drive, Suite 201
Milwaukee, Wisconsin 53212 USA

CHOOSE YOUR OWN NIGHTMARE™ is a trademark of Bantam Doubleday Dell Books
for Young Readers, a division of Bantam Doubleday Dell Publishing Group, Inc.

© 1995 by Edward Packard. Cover art and illustrations © 1995 by Bantam Books.
All rights reserved. Published by arrangement with Bantam Doubleday Dell Books
for Young Readers, a division of Bantam Doubleday Dell Publishing Group, Inc.

Printed in the United States of America

1 2 3 4 5 6 7 8 9 99 98 97 96

For Tini, as promised

WARNING!

You have probably read books where scary things happen to people. Well, in *Choose Your Own Nightmare,* you're right in the middle of the action. The scary things are happening to you!

Meg's scary party is getting way out of hand. And her mom is a terrible chaperon—in fact, she may be a witch!

Fortunately, while you're reading along, you'll have chances to decide what to do. Whenever you make a decision, turn to the page shown. The thrills and chills that happen to you next will depend on your choices.

Choose carefully. This is one party that can last forever.

What a night! Rain, thunder, and lightning. But you're going to have a great Halloween anyway—without even leaving your building!

You're on your way to a big party in Meg Robinson's apartment on the twelfth floor. Meg just moved into your building. You don't know her very well and were surprised that she asked you to come. She probably just wants to make new friends, you think.

Another thing that's great about Halloween this year is your costume—you're dressed as a panther. You admire yourself in the floor-to-ceiling mirror as you wait for the elevator.

Boom! A loud crack of thunder startles you as the elevator door slams open. Oh! That weird Mr. Grimaldin from the thirteenth floor is standing inside.

"Hurry up! I'm late!" he snaps.

You get in and stand as far away from him as you can. He reminds you of a wicked Santa Claus: short and fat, with a bushy beard, narrow green eyes, and rosy cheeks.

Tonight Mr. Grimaldin is creepier than usual. He's dripping wet from the rain—it almost looks as if he's melting.

Turn to page 2.

2

"What an interesting design," he hisses.

It takes you a second to realize he means the pattern you've drawn on your face with your red grease pencil.

"It's supposed to protect against evil spirits, Mr. Grimaldin. I saw it on a TV documentary," you say.

"You can't wear something like that on Halloween!" he cries, his eyes glaring.

Just then the elevator door opens. What perfect timing! You rush out as Mr. Grimaldin sputters something about evil. Why is he so upset, anyway?

You ring Meg's bell, and her door creaks open. It's very dark inside. When you walk in, the door slams shut. You jump, even though you know someone's done it to scare you. You look around but don't see anyone.

You've heard that Meg's dad does special effects for the movies. The slamming door must be one of his ideas for the party.

Go on to the next page.

A row of small plastic jack-o'-lanterns on the floor leads you into the darkened living room. More pumpkins, big and little, real and plastic, provide the only light. They're everywhere! So are lots of kids in costumes. To your left is a cowboy. And in front of you stand a couple of kids dressed like crayons. Off to the side you see the shadowy figure of a woman. That must be Meg's mom, you think.

Music is playing, but almost nobody is dancing. In a dark corner kids are bobbing for apples.

"Spooky, huh?" says a hairy werewolf with dangling gold earrings. It's your friend Laurie!

"Boy, am I glad to see you," she says. "I was starting to think you weren't coming." She steps back to get a good look at you. "Cool costume," she says.

"It took me a while to get my face done right," you say.

Turn to page 4.

4

Laurie leads you over to the food table. Pizza, potato chips, cheese puffs, a cake, and a big bowl of candy greet your hungry stare. At both ends of the table are plastic tubs shaped like pumpkins, full of crushed ice and cans of soda. What a great spread!

Shining at you from smack in the middle of the table is the biggest jack-o'-lantern you've ever seen. As you reach for a cheese puff, the pumpkin's candle flares up, making it seem to glare right at you.

Maybe they're overdoing this pumpkin stuff, you think nervously.

"Well, well, it's the witch's cat," says Meg from behind you. She must be talking about your panther costume.

You whirl around. Meg is dressed as Little Bo-Peep. She's wearing a flouncy, old-fashioned dress. In one hand she holds a shepherd's staff.

"Hi, Meg," you say. What a dumb costume, you think.

"Meg's got something special planned," says the cowboy, who is standing beside her. It's your friend Peter.

Go on to the next page.

"It's about time you got here," Meg says. "I thought I'd have to start the spell without you."

"A spell? What spell?" you ask.

She puts down the staff and pulls a small black notebook out of her skirt pocket. "Mr. Grimaldin dropped this near the front door last week. It's got magic spells in it!"

"That's stealing. And anyway, you're making this all up," you say.

"It's borrowing. And I don't make things up!" she exclaims.

"Stop arguing and try it out," says Peter. He always likes to make peace and get things done.

"This way," says Meg. You, Laurie, and Peter follow her down a dark hallway into the dining room. No one else joins you.

There's another big jack-o'-lantern with a nasty expression sitting on the dining room table. You feel uneasy. Do they have to put them in *every* room?

When you are all in the room, Meg draws a big chalk circle with six pie-shaped sections on the floor, each with a symbol in it.

Turn to page 10.

6

"Do you think that was a real witch?" Laurie asks nervously.

"Of course not! It was a trick. The wires got crossed or overloaded or something," says Peter.

"Where's Mrs. Robinson?" asks Laurie.

"And where's Meg?" you ask, looking around.

Meg rushes in. She's crying. "I can't find my mom and there's smoke in the hall. And the phones aren't working so I can't dial 911 for help!"

You look around. Everyone else has left.

"We've got to find Meg's mother," says Peter. "She might be hurt."

"We've got to go get help," says Laurie.

You know you have to do both these things. The only question is, who does what?

If you go with Peter and Meg to find Meg's mother, turn to page 19.

If you go with Laurie to get help, turn to page 7.

"Laurie and I will go get help," you tell Peter. "You and Meg look for Mrs. Robinson."

"Good thinking," says Peter. He and Meg head for the dining room. You and Laurie follow the row of pumpkins to the front door.

You're in such a rush to get out that you let the door slam and lock behind you before you realize the lights are out in the hallway. It's very dark.

"Oooh, this is scary," whispers Laurie.

"Don't panic," you say. "There's an explanation for everything." Despite your bravado, your heart is beating faster.

"Okay, how do you explain this?" asks Laurie, waving her arms around.

"This is an old building with old wiring," you say. "Those Halloween tricks just used up too much power, like Peter said."

"You're sure the witch wasn't real?" Laurie whispers.

"Of course not! Mr. Robinson does special effects for movies and TV. Something must have gone wrong." But you know something about witches, and she sure *looked* real, you think uneasily.

Turn to page 40.

8

You wonder why it hasn't done any good yet.

"The design doesn't always work," murmurs Mr. Grimaldin, as if he can read your mind. "It depends on how powerful the evil is."

You feel defenseless against this witch. But Mr. Grimaldin seems to be here to protect you, too. Is there some kind of connection between him and your parents?

Mr. Grimaldin smiles.

"What are you two *talking* about?" asks Laurie impatiently.

You shush her. "How can we get out of here?" you ask.

Mr. Grimaldin grimaces. "Why don't you stay awhile?" he says. "You can come to the Halloween party in this apartment. That's why I'm here. And I'll call for help for your friends."

"I knew we should have gone down in the elevator!" whispers Laurie.

Maybe she's right. But you still don't trust that elevator.

Turn to page 65.

"We've got to get out of here!" you exclaim.

"You're better off here," says Walter. "The cemetery is dangerous. We're staying in here until the sun comes up. Then we can get out of the cemetery safely."

"Walter's right," says Meg.

"What about finding Peter? He's not here," you remind her.

"Maybe he is," says Walter. "We heard footsteps when we came in. They were heading for the back."

Meg brightens. "See, he *did* come here."

"I can give you one of our extra candles," says Walter.

"What if it's not him?" you say.

"Who else could it be?" asks Meg. You look at each other fearfully.

Maybe you should stay with Walter and his friends. If Peter is in the back, he'll hear your voices and come out.

But what if he fell in the dark and is lying there unconscious? Or what if he needs your help to get away from the witch?

If you yell for Peter to come out, turn to page 46.

If you go look for Peter, turn to page 43.

10

"My mom would kill me if I wrote on our wood floor with chalk," you whisper to Laurie. She nods nervously.

"I'm going to do a spell for Halloween presents," Meg says. "We'll have the best Halloween ever."

She puts a lighted candle in the middle of the circle. Then she takes some pebbles from her pocket and tells you all to hold hands around the candle.

As you do, you see Meg's mom's shadow on the wall. You're glad she's keeping tabs on this. What Meg is doing might not be safe.

Meg chants a lot of gibberish and throws the pebbles into the circle.

Nothing happens. You knew she was faking.

"What went wrong, Meg?" asks Laurie.

"Nothing," says Meg in an annoyed tone.

Suddenly the shadow on the wall slides down onto the floor and into the circle. It's not Meg's mom after all! But what is it? It's whirling around and creating a big dark cloud. Wow! Another of Meg's dad's special effects. What a cool trick!

Turn to page 38.

12

"In a minute," you say, before Laurie can mention bobbing for apples.

The creature frowns, and its spiky hair droops toward you. It really is spiky. You step back.

"You must choose soon," says Spiky, all four eyes glaring at you, "or pay the penalty!" As it swirls away, its cloak brushes your legs.

"Ouch!" The cloak is spiky, too. You lean against the piano to rub your leg. You've just realized something.

"Laurie, we've got to be very careful. I don't think these people are in costume," you whisper.

"Sure they are," she says. "Just look at them."

"Hee-haw! Going to pay the penalty?" brays the piano-playing donkey. "It's been too long since someone paid the penalty! And I'm hungry!"

Its ears are large, filthy, and pointy. A long pink tongue lolls wetly out of its mouth.

Laurie backs quickly away. "You're right!" she gasps, grabbing your arm. "How can we get out of here?"

Turn to page 41.

When the elevator doesn't come after a few minutes, you and Laurie head for the stairs.

You start down with Laurie right behind you. Suddenly you both slip. You grab for the railing, but it's too late, and you tumble forward, landing in a heap at the bottom.

"Ow!" you groan. You don't think you've broken anything, but you sure feel battered.

Laurie gingerly holds up some pieces of candy corn. "This is what we slipped on. It's all over the stairs!"

"Kids going home from Meg's party must have scattered it," you say.

"Or it's a trick, just like the witch promised," says Laurie, shivering.

"Laurie, that was no witch, believe me!" you exclaim. But you can't help feeling more than a twinge of doubt.

You and Laurie get up and open the stairwell door. You're on the eleventh floor, and here the hall lights are working.

At the first apartment you're about to ring the bell when you see that the door is ajar. A pumpkin-shaped sign on it reads: Welcome Halloween Trick-or-Treaters!

Turn to page 62.

14

"I don't know," you say nervously. "Maybe something got her. Like a ghost in the tall grass!" Or maybe you're right about her, and she's making sure something gets *you,* you think.

Then you realize that you and Peter are standing next to a crumbling vault covered with twisting vines. What if something dead inside there decides to come out? You've read that ghosts can wake up and roam the earth on Halloween.

You and Peter tense up. Something is moving toward you through the mist.

You're ready to run when you see it's Meg. She's racing toward you, looking over her shoulder.

"Help! It's following me," she whimpers, pointing behind her. Around the corner of the vault floats a pale woman wearing a long, ragged dress. She must be a ghost from the vault!

Meg rushes up to you. "Don't let it get me!"

Peter waves his arms. "I command you to go away!" he yells at the ghost.

Turn to page 66.

"Gosh, it really suits you, Mr. Grimaldin," Laurie whispers.

Mr. Grimaldin must be a grimalkin—a witch's helper who can turn into a cat. But who is his witch? you wonder.

The cat taps you on the shoulder with its paw. "Or, *mmeow,* you could, *mmeow,* dance."

"Hurry up!" yowls the spiky-haired creature.

"Which one should we pick?" whispers Laurie.

"I don't know!" you whisper back.

You've got to choose, and fast, but you don't see how either activity will get you out safely. But Mr. Grimaldin must know what he's talking about.

If you decide to draw your face design on all the creatures, turn to page 68.

If you decide to dance, turn to page 26.

Both the man and the woman are staring at you eagerly. Almost hungrily.

"We've got eight children so far," says the man.

The way he says it makes it sound as if the children aren't theirs, just some kids who wandered in—as you and Laurie did.

You both start to back up.

"We have to go now," says Laurie shakily.

"Sorry, but we need to get help," you say.

"You can't leave. You took our candies," says the woman angrily.

"Here, take them back," says Laurie. The two of you quickly empty your pockets. Then you turn and run!

"Stop!" yells the man, but you race out.

"What were they? Ghosts?" cries Laurie.

"Never mind about that now. Let's get to another floor *fast*!" you gasp.

Laurie hits the elevator call button just as the hall lights go out. You're in the dark again!

"If it doesn't come in two seconds, we're taking the stairs!" you cry.

If you wait for the elevator, turn to page 82.

If you go down the stairs, turn to page 73.

"It must be Peter!" you exclaim, moving forward.

Meg grabs your arm. "How do we know it's him?"

"She's right!" whispers Walter. "Let's all hide in the corners, where the shadows are deepest."

"Okay," you say quickly. You and Meg head for one corner, and after blowing out the candle, Walter and his friends crouch in another.

You hold your breath. The footsteps are getting closer. Whoever it is will turn the corner any second.

Someone is standing in the passageway!

Is it Peter? It's so dark, you can't see.

"Hello, are you there?" calls a familiar voice.

It's Peter! You rush up to him.

"I ran to the back when I heard some people come in. And I fell and hurt my knee," he tells you. You tell him it was only a group of kids your age. As you're talking, you realize no one else is with you.

"Meg, it's Peter!" you shout. Why is she still hiding in the corner?

Turn to page 74.

18

Two floors above you, a door suddenly opens. "I think they're nearby." You recognize the raspy voice. They're coming after you!

You jump up to open the door beside you.

It won't budge.

"Quick! Let's try the next floor down," you whisper.

You hear voices calling you. They're coming down the stairs!

You hurry quietly down to the next floor. The door won't open there, either.

"I see them!" cries a voice. "Hey! Wait!"

You and Laurie race down several flights of stairs until you don't hear the voices anymore.

"We lost them," Laurie pants.

"They're just slow. Let's try some more doors before they catch up," you say.

None of the doors opens.

You feel as if you've been running down more flights than there are floors in the building. Your legs hurt, and you're so out of breath you have to hold on to the railing to keep from falling.

Turn to page 50.

You decide to help Meg and Peter look for Meg's mom. If she's lying hurt somewhere, it will take all three of you to get her to safety. Laurie can easily go for help by herself.

"Mrs. Robinson might need first aid," Peter says. He's taken a course in that.

"C'mon!" Meg cries, leading you back into the smoke—the last place she saw her mom. She tells you there's no real fire. The smoke is from a dispenser in the pumpkin that blew up.

Tears are running down Meg's face. And down yours, too, from the smoke. Meg's parents should be more careful about their Halloween tricks. Don't they know how unhealthy smoke is?

The smoke is so thick and irritating that you can't see where Meg is leading you. Finally you enter a large, beautiful, smoke-free room. The door slams shut behind you.

"Here they are, Mother," says Meg. She has a funny smirk on her face. Her tears are gone.

Turn to page 75.

"Do you suppose—" Laurie begins.

"No!" you interrupt. "The wiring in the indicator went bad because of all the special effects, that's all."

"That must be it," agrees Laurie.

The elevator keeps clicking smoothly along. You begin to relax.

"It has to stop when it gets to the lobby," you say. "We'll have the doorman call for help and let him know this elevator is out of order. He can take us to our floors on the service elevator."

"Right," says Laurie.

You stand there staring at each other as the elevator keeps going—and going—and going.

Just as you begin to get jumpy again, the elevator comes to a smooth stop. The door glides open onto a hallway.

Even though it's not working properly, you both automatically glance up at the floor indicator.

"Minus thirteen!" exclaims Laurie. "Where is *that*?"

"It's a mistake," you say. "Maybe it's plus thirteen." Mr. Grimaldin's floor!

Turn to page 58.

The sheets must not be hers. You hope the owner is someone normal and comes soon!

The elevator opens again. You don't see anyone get out. But you do hear chirpy sounds.

Your heart sinks. It's *not* someone normal.

The witch lurches as if something has bumped her. "You!" she exclaims, as one of the sheets fills out and floats off the table.

"G-G-Ghosts," stammers Laurie. "I-I-Invisible."

Another sheet fills out and rises. Then another and another.

There are so many! You'll never get away now.

"Stay out of my way, you little twerps!" the witch snarls, stuffing her laundry into the dryers.

"Chirr-chirp?" The ghosts are floating around Mrs. Robinson—they seem to be asking her something.

"They are *mine,* they are under *my* curse. Playing tricks on them until they die is my treat to myself for Halloween," Mrs. Robinson says, her voice rising.

Turn to page 78.

You want to avoid any possible cemetery ghosts. "They're part of the witch's bag of tricks," you say. Animals in the forest are not. You hope.

"Then let's hurry," says Peter, starting off.

The woods is not as dark as you expected. Moonlight filters through the treetops, and you can see well enough to move along at a good clip.

"It's so quiet!" whispers Meg.

It's more than quiet, you realize. There isn't a sound except for the soft crunch of your footsteps. Nothing moves. Not even a leaf rustles. A chill runs up your spine.

Then you see a cracked and moldy headstone jutting out from behind a tree. And another old headstone half hidden by a bush.

"Oh no! We're in the cemetery!" cries Meg.

You're exactly where you didn't want to be! Ghosts can come after you here!

The witch has tricked you again.

You all start to run. Panting, you reach the edge of the woods and stop to catch your breath. The cemetery gate is only a short distance away.

Turn to page 49.

24

Are the witch and her Halloween curse real after all? And is Meg's mom the witch? Maybe she just wants to make sure you enjoy the Halloween party. But how good can the party be when everyone else has gone home? And she's acting very weird.

Then you notice her long, jagged red nails.

Clara gets up and walks toward you as if she knows what you're thinking.

"It's Halloween until midnight!" she exclaims. Suddenly she stops. "What is that *thing* on your face?" she snarls.

"I saw it on a TV documentary about a Pacific Islands tribe," you tell her. "They paint it on their faces to ward off evil."

She hands you a washcloth. "Wipe it off!"

"Why?" you ask. You wonder where she got the washcloth so fast.

"Now!" screams Clara. You drop the washcloth in surprise. Even Meg looks startled.

Turn to page 69.

You don't really want to sit around waiting. And you know that people often start their laundry at night and pick it up the next morning.

"Okay, let's go through the alley," you say.

You pry open the service door and see that you're in luck. It's not raining or thundering anymore. This was definitely the right move.

But the alley looks awful. It's narrow and dark and crammed with stacks of old newspapers, garbage bags, and plastic recycling bins full of bottles and cans. Phew! It's smelly, too.

There's not much space to walk, so you and Laurie have to go single file.

"Help! I'm stuck!" cries Laurie.

You turn and see that she's caught between two large garbage bags. "If I got through there, so can you."

"They *moved,*" she whispers.

"Garbage bags can't move!" you exclaim.

"Just help me get out!" she yells.

Turn to page 47.

You tell Spiky that you and Laurie will dance. It's your best bet. If you can dance over to the door, maybe you can escape.

"They're going to dance!" Spiky yells.

"Oh, goody goody," says the donkey, starting to slobber onto the piano keys. "Nobody lasts long doing that!" The donkey begins to play jangly, off-key music.

"I can't dance to that!" hisses Laurie.

"Do it anyway! Just keep moving toward the door!" you hiss back.

Spiky glowers at you. "Dance! Now!"

You and Laurie start to dance, but badly. It's not easy with this awful music. But the important thing is to get out of here.

The other creatures move back as you whirl clumsily around. Wham! You hit a jack-o'-lantern. It quivers for a second, then crashes onto the floor. Its scary smile is smashed, and the tiny flashlight that kept it lit goes out.

"Ooooh," says the crowd of creatures. But they don't try to stop you.

Maybe you should hit some more pumpkins. You catch Laurie's eye just as she "accidentally" knocks one over. You both grin.

Turn to page 64.

Peter's idea is a good one. The service elevator is right outside. You'll be home in a jiffy.

You also start to cough and ask for water. "And I need to wash off my face design," you sputter.

Clara laughs, then tells Meg to take you and Peter to the kitchen. "But don't forget—Halloween lasts until midnight. You can't escape it!"

In the kitchen, Meg puts out two glasses and hands you a roll of paper towels. Peter turns on the tap. "I want to let the water get really cold."

He's inching toward the service door. A huge garbage bag, packed full and tied, stands beside it.

To make sure Meg doesn't notice what Peter is doing, you fill your glass and gargle noisily. "It tastes so good after all that smoke!" you say.

"Peter, what are you doing?" asks Meg, glancing over at him.

"I'm going home," he says, opening the door. You run after him. The elevator is right there.

Turn to page 83.

28

You decide to take the path out of the cemetery. There's no point in your being caught by a Halloween ghost, too. You're so close to home, you can quickly get help to find Peter.

If Peter is still alive.

And *if* you get home.

Meg comes with you. "I'm afraid to look for Peter by myself," she tells you.

Is she telling the truth? She might just be keeping tabs on you for the witch. But you can hardly blame her for not wanting to stay in the cemetery by herself. Maybe you misjudged her.

The path leads up a hill. When you finally reach the top, you know you made the right decision.

"It looks like we're in the park," you say. "We'll be home in a few minutes!"

You step forward—and drop into a hole.

"Aarrgh! Ugh!" The hole is about six feet deep, with loose, clingy dirt in the bottom.

Meg's frightened face appears above you. "Here, take my hand," she says, giving you a pull up.

Turn to page 57.

Turn to page 57.

"Let's hide," says Laurie.

That's just what you were thinking. Who knows who—or what—is in that elevator? Better to be safe than sorry.

You wedge yourselves into a dusty corner behind the steam pipes.

"I hope it's not the witch," whispers Laurie.

The elevator opens. A woman dressed just like the witch steps out. Her fingernails are bloodred. You huddle farther back into your corner. She won't know you're here if you're quiet.

Unless she knows already.

Then you see her face. It's Meg's mother! She's the witch!

She lights up a cigarette and starts taking out her laundry from the washers—one long black dress after another, then black capes, then some tall, pointy black hats. You wonder how they managed to keep their shape.

Puffing rings of smoke, Mrs. Robinson opens a dryer. She looks annoyed. She hauls out a bunch of white sheets and throws them on the laundry table. Then she does the same with the other dryers.

Turn to page 22.

30

"The alley is too dangerous," you tell Laurie. "Let's wait for someone to pick up their wash."

Laurie agrees, but only because she doesn't want to go through the alley alone.

You sit on the bench by the sorting table. It's very warm in the room—and the washers and dryers are very loud.

"Who does their laundry on Halloween anyway?" mutters Laurie. You can tell she's afraid something is going to happen.

So are you. But what can the witch try here?

Vroom! Vroom! Vroom! The washers start shaking from side to side, making even more noise.

"Yikes!" exclaims Laurie.

"Relax. It's not the witch. The washers are on the final spin cycle." You know that from helping out your mom.

The washers come to a stop. Good. Someone will definitely come soon.

Five minutes later, the dryers stop. In the silence you hear the clank of the service elevator.

Turn to page 29.

You keep your bike down here, but you don't remember the place being so dark. Did someone turn off the lights? And why did the elevator fall anyway? Is Meg's mom really a witch after all?

"We can get out through the basement door," says Peter. You and Meg follow him down the pitch-black hall. It seems longer than it should be, maybe because you have to feel your way.

Then there's no wall anymore, and you feel a slight breeze.

"Hey! We're outside," says Peter in surprise. "We must have taken the wrong turn for the door and come out through this tunnel instead."

None of you knew there was a tunnel.

"We must be in Riverside Park," says Peter. You're only a block from home.

The three of you begin walking. It's pretty dark, and the air is chilly. You wish you were wearing something besides your panther costume.

Turn to page 61.

32

You press the button for the ground floor. The elevator glides down and opens on the lobby. Fred, the doorman, is astonished to see you.

"That elevator's been out of order all night," he tells you.

"You're telling us!" you gasp. You're not getting back into that thing until it's fixed.

Fred can't take you up on the service elevator because it's stuck on a high floor. The repairman is supposed to be here any minute.

Fred says he'll ring your parents on the intercom and tell them you're okay. "Sit down," he suggests. You and Laurie head for a sofa.

"Who's that?" whispers Laurie, pointing to a man slumped in a chair. His hat is pulled down over his face.

The man sits up and removes his hat. You realize with a start that it's Meg's father.

"Say, were you kids at my daughter Meg's party?" he asks.

"Uh-huh," says Laurie.

"How did you like the special effects?"

"They were, uh, really great," Laurie says.

"I'm glad to hear that. I do them for movies and TV, you know." He grins at you.

Turn to page 36.

It's too dangerous to ride around in a broken elevator, you tell Laurie. "We don't know where we'll wind up!" you exclaim.

You walk down the corridor. Every door but one has a Halloween decoration or a sign saying Trick-or-Treaters Welcome! on it.

You knock on the door with no Halloween decorations or signs.

"Who is it?" asks a pleasant voice.

"We live in the building. We need help!"

"Please come in." The door opens.

Laurie sighs with relief. You both enter, and the door closes behind you.

"Yow!" It's Mr. Grimaldin! He looks very angry.

"You thieves stole my book!" he yells. His fat cheeks are bright red.

"We didn't steal it—Meg did!" you cry.

"It's true, it was Meg!" Laurie exclaims. She tells him what happened in Meg's apartment.

Mr. Grimaldin glares at you for a long time. Then his expression softens. "I believe you are telling the truth," he says.

"We just want to go home," says Laurie. Tears roll down her cheeks.

Turn to page 34.

34

Mr. Grimaldin sighs. "That is not easy. The evil witch's curse is very powerful. She stole my powers with my book and added them to hers, but used them for evil, not good."

So Meg's mom *is* a witch, and the curse is real! You and Laurie are in deep trouble! Then you realize that Mr. Grimaldin must be a good guy. You ask if he can help you.

"Yes and no." He gazes at you thoughtfully. "Are you *sure* you saw your face design on a TV documentary?" he asks.

"It was my parents' idea," you admit.

Mr. Grimaldin nods. "Your parents were wise. I did not know it was their idea when I saw you earlier in the elevator."

You know that using magic on Halloween if you're not a witch can get you in big trouble. That's why you can't escape the witch's punishment—Meg tricked all of you into taking part in her spell.

You're not a witch. But the fact is, though few people know it, your parents are. Good witches. You don't have your own powers yet, but they've told you it's okay for you to wear a protective face design on Halloween.

Turn to page 8.

You can't escape! But just then you hear the sounds you've been waiting for—lots of squeaks. The rats living in the cemetery have smelled the crumbs and come to eat them.

The rats jump on the skeletons' feet and leg bones and start chewing them, in search of more crumbs. To your delight, the skeletons are so busy trying to get rid of the rats that they don't notice you are all taking off for the cemetery gate.

Clang! The gate opens. Clang! It shuts. At last you're out! You look back and gasp. The cemetery is gone. You're in the park now, only a block from home.

Peter looks at his watch. "It's midnight!" You're safe at last!

Unless this is the next trick. You look at Peter anxiously. "Is it *really* midnight?" you ask.

The tower clock by the park zoo begins to toll. You listen as it belts out twelve peals.

Halloween is over. No more curses. And no more witches.

At least until next year.

The End

36

You and Laurie get up off the couch.

"Something wrong, kids?" Mr. Robinson asks with a smile.

"We have to see Fred," you say.

"Nice talking with you," says Mr. Robinson, and puts the hat back over his face.

Meg's dad seems okay, but you don't want to take any chances. "We can hang around Fred until midnight," you whisper to Laurie.

There's a jack-o'-lantern on the front desk. You don't think it was there before. It looks just like the ones at Meg's party.

"Something wrong, kids?" Fred asks with a smile.

That's when you realize there isn't a single other person in the lobby. It seems strange.

"Where did you get the pumpkin?" asks Laurie.

"Oh, we've got lots of them," Fred says.

You look around. There are two on the mail desk, and one on each of the little tables by the sofas. You must have been too tired to notice them before.

"Mr. Robinson was *very* generous," says Fred. "He donated over fifty."

Turn to page 81.

You're trying to figure out how Meg's dad did it when a woman in a long black dress emerges from the cloud. You can't see her face, but you can sure hear her furious voice.

"Wretched humans! Meddling where you don't belong on Halloween! Your sentence is death!"

This trick is getting too scary, you think. But somehow you can't move. Neither can the others.

"You are condemned to die . . . by Halloween!" She starts to laugh.

"Wait a minute! What do you mean?" cries Peter.

"Simple, you simpleton! You are all to be punished with Halloween!" she snarls.

Peter frowns. "You mean trick or treat?"

The witch smacks her lips and cackles nastily. "That's right, sonny. My witch tricks! I'll play them all on you. That will be *my* treat!"

She waves a hand with long, jagged red fingernails at all of you.

"If you can keep alive until midnight, you will be free. But you won't be able to!" She laughs again. "Nobody ever is!"

Turn to page 67.

"Let's go look for him," you say to Meg.

She starts back into the fog. You grab on to her sleeve so you won't lose her again.

In the thick mist you keep stumbling on the bumpy ground. You don't see tombstones until you walk into them. They are old and moldy and cracked.

"Wait! This is where Peter disappeared," Meg says, stopping.

"How do you know?" It all looks the same to you.

She points into the fog. "It was right by that little house. See, there's a light in the window." You look. It's a house all right. You must have missed it when you were fleeing from the ghost.

"Peter might have gone there for help," you say. "Or maybe whoever lives there captured him!"

As you approach the house, you have the feeling that someone, or some*thing,* is behind you. You tell yourself you're imagining things.

Close up, you see that the house is made of stone, with a border of carved stone flowers around the door.

Turn to page 63.

40

"Meg made a real mess of things!"

"She did," you agree.

Then you and Laurie smell smoke. It's seeping into the hallway from under the apartment door.

You'd better get help fast!

"Do you think it's safe to take the elevator?" asks Laurie.

You don't know. At your school fire drills, they always tell you never to take an elevator if there is a fire. But there's no fire anywhere near the elevator.

"Let's try," you say. You feel your way along the wall in the dark until you touch the elevator call button. You press it hard.

Will the elevator come? Or is it out of whack, too?

Maybe you should take the stairs. You can see a light in the stairwell—the wiring must still be okay there. And you'd only have to make it to the next floor and then knock on someone's door.

If you take the elevator, turn to page 82.

If you go down the stairs, turn to page 13.

You're wondering the same thing. The only door has two other spiky-haired creatures standing guard. You can't escape.

"I think we have to choose an activity," you tell Laurie.

"Let's bob for apples," she says.

"Laurie, if you paid attention, you would see that no bobbers have come out of the water since we came in!" you hiss.

Beneath her werewolf makeup, her face goes pale.

"I'm back!" shouts the four-eyed creature. Everyone stops partying to stare. Everyone, that is, except the apple-bobbers. They're not even moving anymore.

"What is your activity?" roars Spiky.

You and Laurie stare at each other in dismay.

"Psst, drawing, *mmeow,* your face design, *mmeow,* on everyone, *mmeow,* is, *mmeow,* good," purrs a familiar voice.

You look up. Sitting on top of the piano is a fat black cat with green eyes.

"Mr. Grimaldin?" you say in amazement.

"Ssh, *mmeow,* I'm in, *mmeow,* costume."

Turn to page 15.

42

"Welcome," says a raspy voice. You both jump.

A tall, thin man walks into the room and slides into one of the chairs. He looks as faded as the furniture.

He's so faded you can almost see through him to the back of the armchair. You must be tired. You blink to clear your vision.

"Did we wake you?" you ask.

He smiles. "Sort of. But I'm glad you did!"

"Do we have some more trick-or-treaters?" asks a woman. You whirl around. She's behind you—tall, thin, and faded looking, too.

"There's an emergency on the twelfth floor. We need to use your phone," says Laurie.

"Now where did I leave the portable phone?" The woman laughs. "Let me think while you help yourselves to some more candy. The children will be out in a minute. They're *so* excited!"

Turn to page 16.

You're not giving up now. If Peter is in this mausoleum, you're determined to find him.

Meg takes the candle from Walter, and the two of you hurry off. Once you turn the corner, all you see ahead and behind you is darkness. And all you hear is the *scrape-scrape* of your footsteps.

The candle doesn't provide much light. Its tiny flame creates flickering shadows on the walls. You hope they're only shadows. The shadow at Meg's party turned into the witch.

You wish you instead of Meg were holding the candle. You still don't trust her. She seems too eager. The stone passageway becomes narrower, and the air turns even more musty, stale, and cold. Maybe she's leading you into a trap.

"Wait. Where are we going?" you whisper.

Meg holds the candle high. You see a set of stone steps heading down.

"That's where all the d-dead p-people are," she says shakily.

"Where else can we look?" you ask. You feel better about Meg. She's as nervous as you are.

Turn to page 53.

44

"That feels good," the creature grumbles. "What is your next activity going to be?"

"What?" you croak. You look at the piano. Mr. Grimaldin is gone. What do you do now?

"Ha ha ha ha!" sneers Spiky. "You didn't think we would let you go, did you? Your next activity better be just as good." Then the creature sits down, closes its four eyes, and falls asleep.

You look around. You've been working so hard you haven't noticed that all the creatures fell asleep right after you drew the design on them.

That makes sense, you realize. The design works against evil. These creatures are only good when they're asleep!

You and Laurie hurry out of the apartment—and there is your dad!

Turn to page 72.

46

"Anybody could be in the back of the mausoleum," you say. "Especially the witch, waiting to play another trick on us!" The smart thing, you decide, is to yell Peter's name. If he's there, he'll come out.

"What if he's hurt and can't answer?" asks Meg.

"It can't hurt to try," you say.

Walter agrees. "Why take more chances than you have to?"

Meg glowers at both of you. "Oh, all right."

"Peter! Are you there? It's us!" the two of you holler over and over. You wait, but there's no answer.

"We have to go look for him," Meg says finally.

"I thought I heard something," you say.

All of you keep very still and listen. And you hear . . . footsteps! Very slow footsteps.

Turn to page 17.

You grab her arm and pull. Nothing happens.

"Oow, it's squeezing me more!"

You grab her other arm and pull harder. It doesn't do any good. She's really stuck!

"I can't breathe," she gasps. "I knew the witch would get me!"

"Laurie, it's only a couple of garbage bags!"

"Urgg . . ." Her face is turning red.

Something is getting her! You've got to help her—fast. But how? You grab a couple of empty bottles from the recycling bin and start smacking the garbage bags.

"What are you doing?" gasps Laurie.

"Hold on!" you cry. You're making big dents in the bags. Now you can wedge a bottle between one of the bags and Laurie. You grab her hands and pull.

"Ouf!" She's out! And taking big, deep breaths.

"Watch out!" You whirl around. The recycling bins are tipping over. Bottles are falling on you!

Turn to page 56.

48

Then you realize only Meg is there.

"Where's Peter?" you ask.

"We got separated. We've got to go back and find him!" she cries.

Something tells you that's a bad idea. If the ghost has Peter, there's nothing you can do for him. And you have a funny feeling that whatever happened to Peter was Meg's fault. She might lead you into the same trap.

Then you notice a path running up out of the cemetery that you weren't able to see before. In the distance you see what looks like the city skyline. The path must lead to the park. You're close to home after all! You can run for help and then go back to look for Peter.

But time may be running out for Peter. Shouldn't you go back and try to find him *now*?

If you decide to look for Peter, turn to page 39.

If you take the path, turn to page 28.

"We made it!" says Peter.

"The witch must have run out of Halloween magic," says Meg.

You gaze into the swirling mist. "No she didn't!" you say, pointing.

"Skeletons!" Meg gasps.

Because they are the same color as the mist, the skeletons are hard to see—but you can tell there are a lot of them. They float between you and the gate.

"How can we get out of this?" you ask.

"Maybe we can't," says Peter.

"I wish I'd never seen Mr. Grimaldin's book!" exclaims Meg.

"It's too late now, Meg," says Peter.

"Psst—pipe down! They've seen us!" you hiss.

One of the skeletons drifts toward you. Its skull gleams in the moonlight. It must be the leader.

"A dance for your Halloween passage," it rasps.

"That doesn't sound so bad," whispers Meg.

"It's the dance of death," you whisper back. "I read it in a book."

Turn to page 80.

50

You're at the bottom door. If it doesn't open . . . you don't want to think about it.

It opens . . . to the basement.

You slam the door behind you and shove the dead bolt home. They won't get through that. You're safe, for the time being anyway.

"Let's go out the service entrance and through the alley," says Laurie. "Then we can circle around to the front door."

"The witch would love that!" you exclaim.

"Yeah, you're right," she says.

"Let's take the service elevator," you say. It's right by the laundry room. It's very noisy because the washers and dryers are going. You glance into the laundry room, but no one is there.

You press the elevator button, but the elevator doesn't come.

"It's not working," you say finally. "But someone will come to collect their laundry sooner or later. We can ride up with them."

"The alley is faster," says Laurie. "It's not that creepy."

If you go through the alley, turn to page 25.

If you wait in the laundry room, turn to page 30.

"Peter and I have to go home," you say. "Our parents are waiting."

"They must be worried by now," adds Peter. "They'll probably be here any minute looking for us."

"Oh, I don't think so," says Mrs. Robinson. "Meg phoned them to say you're sleeping over. We're going to have such fun!"

Then she looks at you. "At least Meg and I are going to have fun."

She is the witch! And she's got you trapped. You have to get out of here. You take out your red grease pencil.

You stoop down and quickly draw your face design on the floor before she can stop you.

"You can't do that here!" shrieks Mrs. Robinson.

"I just did, and I can draw it on your face, too!" you say. Meg and her mother hastily back away.

"The party's over! Go home!" shouts Mrs. Robinson.

You leave before she can change her mind. It's easy to find your way out of the apartment now. There's no smoke anywhere.

Turn to page 76.

52

You hear coins clinking onto the floor as you hurry into the service elevator.

"Come back here!" shrieks the witch, throwing a quarter at you. Just in time, the door shuts. In seconds, you're in the lobby. The little ghosts grab your sheets and zoom out the main entrance before you can even thank them.

"What's their hurry?" asks Laurie.

You look at your watch. It's midnight. Halloween is over. They had to get out. As for you and Laurie, you're saved!

At the front desk, Fred the doorman tells you that the main elevator is finally back in working order. "What a night this has been!" he exclaims.

You and Laurie sigh. "It sure has!" you chorus.

As you head for the main elevator, you think this must be a Halloween dream. How else can you explain being rescued by a bunch of chirping little ghosts?

You're kind of afraid to pinch yourself, though.

The End

"Why don't we call Peter's name?" suggests Meg.

"Peter! Are you there?" you both yell.

Silence. You yell again. More silence.

Then you hear a faint moan. You look at each other. Is it a ghost, or is it Peter?

"What should we do?" whispers Meg.

"Peter! It's us!" you yell as loud as you can.

"H-Help . . . ," comes a weak groan.

"Wait!" you shout, but she's already rushing down the narrow stone stairs. You stumble after her.

Someone's down there—but is it Peter?

It is Peter. Meg is helping him up.

"I hit my head," says Peter. One side of his face is caked with blood. "Something was chasing me, and I fell down the stairs." He swallows. "I'm sure glad to see you," he adds.

You're glad to see him, too, but you wonder where the *something* is. If it's waiting for you in here, you're in trouble.

The walls of the room are made of large, square stone tablets. Each tablet has a person's name on it. Their coffins must lie just behind the tablets!

Turn to page 70.

"I'll never do it again!" cries Meg.

"You're right about that!" The witch twists Meg's arm. "I think I'll begin with you, Little Bo-Peep!"

Meg faints.

There's a knock at the door.

"Who's there?" croons the witch sweetly. The door starts to open.

"Stop! Go away! That door is locked!" she yells. The door opens all the way. It's Mr. Grimaldin. He's carrying the small black book Meg borrowed.

"Let the children go," he says, flipping through the book.

"Never!" shrieks the witch, pointing her red fingernails at him. Streaks of fire shoot out of them, heading straight toward Mr. Grimaldin!

Mr. Grimaldin chants something. The streaks of fire dribble to the ground and disappear.

He goes on, pointing a finger at the witch:

"Your power is of the hour,
And the hour is done!"

Turn to page 77.

You duck just in time. "Let's get out of here!" you cry, pushing Laurie ahead of you.

The bottles roll after you down the alley, tripping you just as you reach the sidewalk.

The Dugans, neighbors who live in your building, happen to be passing by. They help you up. You feel a stab of fear when you see that their two girls are wearing witch costumes.

"Tick or teeth!" says the littler one.

"Not now, dear," says Mrs. Dugan.

"That's okay," says Laurie. The two of you search your pockets and give each child a quarter.

"Happy Halloween!" you say. *Someone* should have one!

The End

You look back into the hole. It's shaped funny, like a long rectangle.

"There are a lot of them," whispers Meg.

Then you realize what the holes are. Newly dug graves! You must still be in the cemetery, in a brand-new section of it. This path is much more dangerous than you thought. You really have to watch your step!

"Follow me," you whisper to Meg. You carefully avoid one new grave after another. Once you get over being scared, it's pretty easy.

Then you see a newly filled-in grave. Curious, you bend over to look at the headstone— and see Peter's name!

"Oh no!" You panic and run, only to find yourself teetering on the edge of another empty grave. Meg grabs you before you fall in.

"Thanks! That was close!"

"I couldn't let you fall in there!" she cries.

You take back every bad thing you ever thought about her. Even though you feel terrible about Peter, you and Meg have to save *yourselves* now.

If you can.

Turn to page 84.

58

But how could that be? You've been going *down* for the longest time. And you were below the thirteenth floor when you started.

The indicator just isn't working properly. You're probably on some lower floor.

"Let's knock on someone's door and get help," you say.

But Laurie wants to stay in the elevator and press the lobby button. "Thirteen is unlucky, and minus thirteen is worse!" she wails.

"I can't believe you're so superstitious!" you exclaim. You know she's thinking about the so-called witch's curse. It's going to be hard to talk her out of this.

On the other hand, taking the elevator to the lobby will solve your problems right away. But because the elevator is not working properly, you suspect that no matter which button you press, it won't take you there.

But you could be wrong.

If you decide to stay on the minus-thirteenth floor, turn to page 33.

If you stay in the elevator and press the button for the lobby, turn to page 32.

The witch's curse is real! That means evil tricks will be played on you no matter where you are. But a cemetery is the worst place to be. You want to get out as fast as possible.

And the fastest way is straight through the graves.

"But there's so much fog," says Meg, when you tell her your decision.

"We won't be in it for long," you say. She doesn't look convinced.

"C'mon," Peter says, starting through the tall grass. You and Meg follow him.

The grass swishes aside with a funny sound as you walk through it. Is someone following you? You look back but see only fog.

You feel nervous. What's the next trick going to be?

And you don't quite trust Meg. You think the witch probably *is* her mother. You're glad you're walking behind her. But the fog is so thick it's hard to see her.

"Meg?" She doesn't answer.

Peter looms out of the fog. "Where did she go?"

Turn to page 14.

Suddenly you stumble over a dead log. When you look up, you see an old cemetery full of weeds below you. The only light comes from the full moon.

This isn't the park.

An eerie mist swirls around the cemetery's cracked and broken headstones. From a nearby tree, an owl hoots softly. All three of you jump.

"How do we get out of here?" cries Meg.

"We have to go through the cemetery to reach that gate," says Peter, pointing to a gate in the distance.

"The cemetery must have evil ghosts," says Meg. She wants to go through the woods that lie to your left to get to the gate.

"But there might be dangerous animals in the woods," says Peter.

They both look at you as if you know what to do.

If you go through the cemetery, turn to page 59.

If you go through the woods, turn to page 23.

62

"Great, we can get some treats and phone for help," says Laurie, pushing open the door.

The foyer is empty. You walk into the living room. Nobody there either. Trick-or-treating must be over. It is kind of late.

Then you see a big bowl of candy on a coffee table. Laurie hurries over and helps herself.

"Helloo! Can we use your phone?" you shout. You scoop up some candy, too.

You look around. The couch and chairs are faded and lumpy. There is something strange about this place. Maybe you should try another apartment.

Turn to page 42.

"This place looks creepy. Should we knock?" asks Meg. The tiny windows are too high to peek into.

"Yes, we want to find Peter," you say firmly. You knock. Then you hold your breath.

"W-W-Who's th-th-there?"

It sounds like another kid! What a relief.

"We're lost. We're looking for a friend in a cowboy costume," you say through the door.

The door creaks open.

"Hi, I'm Walter," says the boy. He's a few inches taller than you. "We got lost, too. We were trick-or-treating," he adds. He's wearing a Dracula costume. Behind him are a boy and a girl dressed as Frankenstein and his bride. They move aside to let you in.

"Are we glad to see you!" you say.

The house is all stone inside as well. There's no furniture, and the only light comes from the candle in the window.

It's very cold and damp. Brrr! Who'd live in this place? "What kind of a house is this?" you ask.

Walter giggles. "Don't you know? It's a mausoleum. Dead people are buried in here."

Turn to page 9.

64

Spiky is the only creature that seems upset as you keep hitting pumpkins.

"Stop that!" it snarls.

Your plan is working. You're much closer to the door. Now you and Laurie dance toward the last pumpkin—the big jack-o'-lantern on the main table, the one with the really mean look.

"Don't!" yells Spiky, running toward you.

You kick at the pumpkin together.

Bull's-eye! But instead of smashing when it hits the ground, the jack-o'-lantern starts rolling toward you.

The creatures all start to run, and so do you and Laurie. You run out the apartment door and slam it behind you. Laurie shoves one of her earrings in the keyhole to jam the lock.

The jack-o'-lantern starts banging so fiercely that the door begins to bulge outward.

"Let's get out of here before that thing breaks the door down!" Laurie cries.

"Here we go again!" you exclaim. "Do we take the elevator or the stairs?"

"Isn't there any other way we can get away?" cries Laurie desperately.

Turn to page 79.

You decide to stay at the party for a few minutes while Mr. Grimaldin calls for help. With Mr. Grimaldin around, it can't be that dangerous.

"You know, I never really liked him, but he's being awfully nice," you whisper to Laurie.

She shrugs. "I guess," she says.

You follow Mr. Grimaldin through the apartment to where the party is being held. The first things you notice are jack-o'-lanterns on buffet tables. The biggest one looks just like the one on the table at the Robinsons' party. It has the same nasty expression.

"What do we do?" you ask Mr. Grimaldin.

"Mingle," he says, and vanishes into the crowd. You're on your own, you realize in dismay.

Many partygoers are dancing to a jumpy tune that a "donkey" is banging out on the piano. Others are bobbing for apples.

"Great costume," you say, pointing to the donkey.

"That bobbing looks like fun," says Laurie.

"Can I help you choose an activity?" asks a creature with four eyes and spiky blond hair.

Turn to page 12.

66

The ghost smiles and keeps on coming. Its teeth are long, dirty, and very sharp. Now it's heading straight for Peter!

You've got to do something fast. Crouching down, you feel around for a rock. As the ghost reaches for Peter with clawlike hands, you run up and jam the rock into its mouth.

"Aaarrgh!" gurgles the ghost. You can see that at least one long curving tooth is broken in half.

"Run!" you shout. The three of you take off. You stop after about a hundred yards. Your heart is pounding, and it's not just from running!

"We're safe now," you gasp. You've read that a cemetery ghost can only travel a little distance from its final resting place.

Turn to page 48.

Boom! The witch disappears in another cloud of smoke. Soon smoke starts to fill the room. You wonder where it's coming from as you cough, your eyes tearing. You don't like Mr. Robinson's special effects. This isn't fun anymore.

"I think the pumpkin exploded!" cries Laurie.

"Follow me out!" yells Peter, taking charge as usual. He leads you all back into the living room.

Peter flicks on the overhead light and tells the surprised partygoers there's some trouble.

"Nothing serious, but it caused a lot of smoke."

It's almost 10:30 anyway, when the party is supposed to end. Most of the kids decide to leave and begin to file out. Peter shuts the dining room door to make sure the smoke doesn't spread.

Turn to page 6.

You decide to draw the face design. It's supposed to protect you against evil. Well, you're surrounded by it!

You tell Spiky that you will decorate every creature's face.

"And her! What will she do?" snarls Spiky, looking at Laurie. Her eyes widen with fear.

You think fast. "She's my assistant," you say.

"Is that so?" sneers Spiky.

"Yes, it is. Here, Laurie, hold my red grease pencil." You put your hand in the pocket of your panther costume to get the pencil.

It's not there.

Oh no! Meg or her mom must have stolen it. Is there anything else you can use?

"Mmmeow." You look up as the cat rolls another grease pencil over to you along the top of the piano. You grab it and hand it to Laurie. Then you ask Spiky to get everyone in line.

Some of the partygoers are ticklish and laugh when you draw on them. They have bumpy, discolored skin and very bad breath.

Spiky is last.

Turn to page 44.

"I want to go home," you say. This is getting too scary.

Peter coughs. "My throat hurts from all that smoke," he complains. "I need a glass of water."

Mrs. Robinson looks at both of you. "What are we going to do with you?"

Nothing, you hope.

"Meg, I thought your friends *liked* Halloween," she says, and starts to laugh.

"I thought they did too!" titters Meg.

As they talk, Peter whispers to you that he's going to leave by the service door in the kitchen.

Maybe you should sneak out with him. You don't know if Mrs. Robinson will just let you go home.

If you go with Peter to the kitchen, turn to page 27.

If you insist on going home, turn to page 51.

"Let's get out of this place and out of this cemetery," you say.

Peter nods. Then you see a light at the top of the stairs.

"It's come back!" whispers Peter.

But it's just Walter and his friends.

"Hi! I see you found Peter," he says as the three of them come marching down the stairs.

"Yes, thank goodness!" you say. "And we are *leaving*. Why don't you come with us?"

"I think you should stay here," says Walter. He points to a big square tablet behind you. "See? It's all ready for you."

You whirl around. In the flickering light of the candle you see your name carved on the tablet.

"Hey! Here's *my* name!" exclaims Peter.

All of a sudden Meg is standing with the other kids. She's smiling.

Then you notice that Walter's phony Dracula teeth are real. Frankenstein and his bride must be real, too!

You and Peter start to back up as the four of them move slowly toward you.

"Trick or treat!" they say in unison.

The End

"Come on, let's go," he says, heading for the waiting elevator.

"Good timing!" says Laurie.

"It works now!" you say in surprise.

Your dad nods. He tells you that Meg and her parents are being evicted. "We don't want people like that here."

You know *you* sure don't!

After you drop Laurie off on her floor, you go home, where your mom is waiting up. You tell your parents everything.

"And Mr. Grimaldin is a *grimalkin*!" you finish. "I wonder what witch he's helping?"

Your parents look at each other and smile. "How do you think we knew where you were?" they ask.

The End

Several seconds go by, but the elevator doesn't come. You and Laurie make a dash for the stairwell and reach it just as the apartment door opens.

You huddle down behind the stairwell door and keep very still. Not only the strange couple but their eight children are after you! You hear their voices as they roam up and down the pitch-dark corridor.

"Come back! We really like you!"

"Take all the candy you want!"

"I guess they took the elevator," says the man's voice.

It's quiet again. They must have gone back inside the apartment.

"I think that was a trick," whispers Laurie.

You tiptoe slowly down two flights of stairs, then sit on the steps to talk.

"It's real," says Laurie. "The curse is real."

Maybe it is, you think.

"How close is it to midnight?" Laurie asks.

You look at your watch. "Not close enough."

"Why don't we just sit here until midnight?" suggests Laurie.

Turn to page 18.

74

Then you see something behind Peter.

It's wearing a swirling black robe and a pointed witch's hat and motioning to you with long, jagged red fingernails. You and Peter freeze.

"This is your final trick!" cackles the witch.

"M-M-Mom? Is this a joke?" croaks Meg from her hiding place.

The witch laughs. "I'm not your m-m-mom! She's in a trance. So is your d-d-dad!"

She leans forward and drags a squirming Meg out of the corner. "So your d-d-dad does special effects! Well, he doesn't know zilch about *real* special effects. Get a load of this!"

She points at the floor with one red fingernail. *Whoosh!* A fire starts to burn in the middle of the floor. Now the witch can see Walter and his friends cringing in the other corner.

"Yum, dessert, too!" she cackles.

"Let us go!" you cry.

"Not a chance! Meg cast that spell, and now you are all in my power!"

Turn to page 54.
Turn to page 54.

Lounging on a red velvet sofa is a woman in a long black dress. In one hand she holds the sort of tapered cigarette holder you sometimes see in old movies. She smiles. It's not a nice smile.

"We're here to rescue you, Mrs. Robinson," says Peter.

"You must be Peter," says Mrs. Robinson. She blows a smoke ring into his face.

Peter starts to cough.

"Call me Clara," she adds.

"Excuse me, but have you ever thought about quitting smoking?" you ask.

Clara rolls her eyes.

You back away. You don't want a smoke ring in your face.

Clara turns to Meg. "Where is your other friend?"

"She went to get help," says Meg, giggling.

"We'll just have to start without her!"

"Start what?" asks Peter.

"Why, Halloween tricks, of course!"

"We thought you were hurt," you say.

"Wasn't that a grand trick?" Clara laughs.

You begin to feel a little afraid.

Turn to page 24.

"I hope the Robinsons never give a party like this again," says Peter as you board the elevator. "It was terrible."

"If they do, I won't go," you say.

"Me neither!" he says.

After Peter gets off, you go home and tell your parents that the Robinsons are bad witches, just as they suspected. Your parents, on the other hand, are good witches.

"We'll get them out of here fast," says your dad, picking up the phone to call some other good witches who live in the building. Then you call Laurie's apartment—she's safe and sound. Her mom has already called the building superintendent, who promised to go to the Robinsons' apartment immediately.

You're glad your mom insisted you wear the face pattern. You won't have your powers for a couple of years yet. Without the pattern, you and your friends would have been totally at the mercy of the witch.

You're almost afraid to wash the pattern off your face before you go to bed. After all, it isn't midnight yet!

The End

With bloodcurdling shrieks, the witch hitches up her long skirts and runs back down into the mausoleum.

"Gotcha!" says Mr. Grimaldin.

Then he tells all of you to go home. "Your Halloween party is over."

He doesn't seem the least bit like the menacing figure you encountered in the elevator earlier. He's a nice person, you decide.

But then his eyes turn so hard and cold that you gasp and quickly step back. So do the other kids.

"If my book is ever borrowed again, you will be on your own," he says.

You hurry out and run all the way home. Meg's teeth don't stop chattering the whole time. And neither do yours and Peter's. One thing's for sure: the only books you'll *ever* borrow again will be from one place—the library!

The End

She looks straight at where you are hiding and laughs. "Heh, heh, you two are going for a nice *hot* ride with my laundry."

You and Laurie shrink back. You're sunk. She knew where you were all the time.

The room is filling up with the chirping little ghosts. Suddenly one is hovering beside you. "Chirp?" it murmurs, moving closer.

Laurie looks as if she's going to pass out.

"Hold on, I think it's friendly," you whisper. Then you see the extra sheets on the table and the thick row of little ghosts between you and the witch. It's worth a try.

You and Laurie tiptoe to the table and each put on a sheet. You're surprised to find you can see even though there aren't any eyeholes.

The ghosts surround you.

"I'm going to get you two now!" cackles the witch. "Let me make sure I've got enough quarters for an extra-long spin." She fumbles in her pocket for some change. Coming up empty-handed, the witch shouts,

"Magic helper, I've got laundry trouble!
Give me quarters on the double!"

Turn to page 52.

Crash! Thump! The jack-o'-lantern contin-
ues to pound. At this rate it'll break through
the door in no time.

There's a rumble and a click, and the elevator door opens. Mr. Grimaldin walks out.

He looks just like he did when you saw him
earlier, except he's carrying a small black
notebook. It must be the one Meg stole. How
did he get it back? you wonder.

"What a Halloween!" he exclaims. "It's still
raining and thundering. And the elevator just
started working properly!"

All of a sudden you realize it's very quiet in
the hallway.

"What are you still doing here? It's late," he
says. "It's already midnight."

Midnight! You're safe!

Laurie leans against the wall and smiles
tiredly. "We'll go home right away," she says.

"Thanks for your help, Mr. Grimaldin," you
say, as you and Laurie step onto the elevator.

He gives you a sly look. "I'm sure next year
will be even better!" he says.

The End

"We don't have a choice," says Peter.

"I have an idea," you say. "Did you take any cookies from the party?" The other two stare at you in amazement.

"It's our only chance," you say mysteriously. Peter fishes out a chocolate-chip cookie from his cowboy outfit. Meg's Bo-Peep pockets have two. You have one. Not much, but they'll have to do.

"Halloween dance!" rumbles the skeleton. The huge empty eye sockets are actually *looking* at you. Then the double row of teeth grate slowly apart in a terrible grimace. It's smiling!

You're shaking, but you have the cookies firmly clutched in your hands as you walk toward the skeleton. It signals to two smaller skeletons, who start tapping on their kneecaps and elbows, producing a rhythm in three-quarter time.

Jerking as if on a string, the skeleton begins to waltz. You waltz back from it, crumbling the cookies onto the ground as you go.

"Dance!" roars the skeleton, lunging closer. You dart back. But it follows quickly after you. Its bony hand reaches out for you—

Turn to page 35.

"Can you ring my parents, please?" you say.

"Sorry, the intercom just went out of order," says Fred.

"Oh," you say. "Let's get out of here," you whisper to Laurie. You both head for the door.

"Where are you going?" calls Fred.

"Back in a minute!" you yell, running out to the sidewalk. The street seems very quiet for Halloween.

"There's a cop," says Laurie, pointing. As you hurry toward him, he turns around. He's carrying a large, glowing jack-o'-lantern.

"Something wrong, kids?" he asks with a smile.

"Oops, we forgot our coats!" you say. You and Laurie rush back into the building.

Fred and Mr. Robinson are waiting for you. Beside them are huge jack-o'-lanterns. As you stare in horror, their carved eyes flare out at you.

You whirl around. The policeman is right behind you. You're trapped!

The three of them surround you and Laurie. And so do the jack-o'-lanterns, gnashing and grinding their jagged pumpkin teeth.

The End

Suddenly the elevator arrives, clanging open in the pitch-black darkness like a room full of light.

You dash inside it. Laurie punches the Close button, and you hit the one for your floor.

Taking the elevator was obviously the best thing to do. You can get help a lot faster. And in the brightly lit car, things don't seem so scary anymore.

"Mrs. Robinson made a pretty good witch," you say.

"And those were good special effects!" agrees Laurie.

"It was a great party until Meg did that spell," you add.

"I kept thinking those pumpkins were all staring at me," Laurie says. You laugh. You'd been thinking the same thing.

"Did we pass your floor?" asks Laurie.

You both glance at the floor indicator. It's blank.

"It must be out of order," you say. You don't know where you are or what floors the elevator is passing. You glance at each other nervously.

Turn to page 21.

Meg dashes after you but trips over the garbage bag. "Wait for me!" she cries. "That's not my mom in there!"

Peter hits the Open button. In a flash, Meg gets up and races onto the elevator.

"Is that person the witch from the party, Meg?" asks Peter.

Meg starts to cry. "I th-think so. She l-looks like my mom. The witch must have her in her power!"

"My dad will know what to do," you say. You wonder if Meg is lying.

Peter presses the button for your floor. The elevator starts to fall! *Whoosh!* You're plunging downward so fast you can't think!

"Help!" you scream. You're going to crash onto the basement floor and be smashed to bits! You can't see, but somehow you hit the red Emergency button.

The elevator jerks to an abrupt stop, and you all tumble onto the floor.

"Ouch!"

"My knee!" But at least you're alive.

The elevator door opens. You're in the basement.

Turn to page 31.

You're so upset about Peter, you don't notice you're standing on the edge of yet another empty grave.

Suddenly, someone pushes you from behind. You fall and land on your stomach with a thud. You're in terrible pain, and you can't move an inch. Did you break your ribs?

"*This* is your grave," comes Meg's voice.

Someone is shoveling dirt on you.

"Help!" you yell.

You hear giggling. It sounds like Meg.

The End

Get ready for your *own* scary party with these frightening tips. Remember to get adult permission first.

* Line the sidewalk that leads to your house or apartment building with luminarias—special paper bags, made just for this purpose, with flashlights or candles inside.

* Carve scary faces into pumpkins and use flashlights instead of candles to light them.

* Make a tape of spooky howls and moans—get your family to help you!—and play it on a hidden tape recorder.

* Rent super-scary movies and have them playing on your TV.

* Drape white sheets over coatracks and chairs. To really scare your friends, have someone in your family crouch down, draped in a sheet—and jump up when your friends walk by!

* Set up a fan behind a curtain, making it move in the "wind."

* Put fake blood on your face and in your hair (first make sure it washes out!) and drip some

on the refrigerator and stove. Ketchup works great.

* Have a few props lying around—a fake hand in the kitchen sink, a fake bloody knife on the stove.

* Fill bowls with different "body parts." Blindfold guests and have them stick their hands into the bowls and tell you what they feel. The grosser the better, like . . .

Monster Eyeballs: peeled grapes
Intestinal Soup: cooked spaghetti floating
  in water
Cat Brains: raw egg yolks
Blended Ear Wax: whipped butter
Popped Pimple Juice: warm yogurt

Have fun!